For the staff and pupils of Hyde Park Infant School, Plymouth
N.D.

For Anna, who opened my eyes to the beauty of things
S.R.

First published 2012 by Walker Books Ltd

87 Vauxhall Walk, London SE11 5HJ

2 4 6 8 10 9 7 5 3 1

Text © 2012 Nicola Davies

Illustrations © 2012 Salvatore Rubbino

The right of Nicola Davies and Salvatore Rubbino to be identified as author and illustrator respectively
of this work has been asserted by them in accordance with the Copyright, Designs and Patents Act 1988.

This book has been typeset in Cold Mountain Sx and Alghera

Printed and bound in China

British Library Cataloguing in Publication Data: a catalogue record for
this book is available from the British Library

978-1-4063-2739-7

www.walker.co.uk

Just Ducks!

Nicola Davies

illustrated by

Salvatore Rubbino

WALKER BOOKS
AND SUBSIDIARIES
LONDON • BOSTON • SYDNEY • AUCKLAND

Quack-quuuack, quack-quaack-quack.
It's the first thing I hear every morning.
The sounds start long and high and get
quicker and lower at the end.
Quack-quuuack, quack-quaack-quack.

I open my bedroom curtains.
Who could be making all that noise?

Ducks, just ducks!
Down on the river
that flows through
the town.

Male ducks
quack so quietly
you have to be close
to hear them.

Female ducks make a
loud quacking to call other
ducks to join them.

At first, there are only two or three of them,
but by the time I've got my clothes on
lots more have arrived and are
preening and splashing
– and quacking! –
in the sunlight.

It doesn't take long for me to eat my breakfast,
but the ducks take ages over theirs!

When they preen,
ducks spread oil,
from a little spot
just under their tails,
all over their feathers
to keep them shiny and
waterproof.

They're STILL eating when I cross the bridge to go to school.

I look down and see them swimming about, dabbling at the surface ...

"Dabbling" is when ducks nibble at the surface of the water with their beaks to get tiny bits of food – small insects and seeds.

and upending
to reach food that's
under water. Brrrr,
it looks so
cold!

"Upending" is when ducks
push their heads right
under the surface to eat
water plants and creatures
like snails.

We visit the ducks on the way
home from school in the afternoon.
When the weather's very cold,
they're still hungry!

Although ducks can't live
on bread alone, it can help to keep
their tummies full when times
are tough.

Ducks need more food when it's cold,
and in some places people feed ducks
on bread in harsh weather.

I go down to the water and
even though they're wild birds,
they come close, just to see
if I've got any food for them!

They're all mallard ducks, so the girl ones,
the "ducks", are streaky browns and buffs.

The female's
quiet colours help her to
hide from danger
when sitting
on her eggs.

The boys, called "drakes", have glossy green heads, neat white collars and a cute little curl on their tails.

They both have a secret patch of blue on each wing, that I see when they stretch or fly.

Drakes don't sit on eggs, so they don't need to be camouflaged.

I like it when the drakes show off their fine feathers to
the ducks, trying to get one to be their girlfriend.

Sometimes the drakes get very excited
and chase a duck in a gang, or fight, splashing in
the water and making a big fuss.

From autumn through winter, drakes try to find a mate in time for spring, when the ducks will be ready to lay their eggs.

In spring, there won't be so many ducks
on the way home, 'cos they'll be busy nesting.
For almost a month, the mother ducks will
sit on their eggs, hidden away,
sometimes in some pretty
funny places.

Mallard ducks make
their nests on
the ground and
lay between 8
and 13 eggs.

Predators like to eat
eggs and ducklings
so mother ducks
hide their nests
carefully.

Last year, one made her nest in our greenhouse!
When the ducklings hatched ...

they had to climb the wall
at the bottom of the garden,
then jump down to follow
their mum to the river.

As soon as their ducklings hatch, mother
ducks get them to water, no matter what,
because they are safer there from cats
and other hungry mouths.

19

But now it's getting dark.
The lights on the bridge begin
to glow and all over town, people are
getting home for tea. It's time for ducks
to find a safe place for the night.

Some sleep under the bridge.

Ducks usually sleep at
night because they can't see
their food in the dark. But they
must sleep somewhere
predators can't reach them.

20

Some fly off to roost in the reeds.

Some float on the water with

heads tucked under wings ...

21

and SOME don't go to bed at all! I know,
because one night at choir practice, we heard them

If there is food to eat and moonlight or street light to see by, ducks will sometimes stay up late, especially when worms come out of their burrows at night.

quacking softly outside the window as they ate worms off the lawn in the dark! Wak-wak-wak-wak-wak-wak-wak.

When I close my curtains on the frosty stars,
the ducks have disappeared. The bridge
is quiet and there's just the sound
of rushing water and the stillness
of the night.

But in the morning they'll be there ...

QUACK QUACK QUACK QUAACK-QUACK

QUACK QUACK QUAACK-QUACK QUACK

ducks, just ducks!
Down on the river
that flows through
the town.

QUACK

QUACK QUACK QUAACK-QUACK

QUACK

Index

Look up the pages to find out about all these duck things.
Don't forget to look at both kinds of words –
this kind and this kind.

Dozens of Ducks

The ducks in this book are mallard ducks which
are found all over Europe, America, Asia,
Australia and New Zealand. But they are only
one of more than 120 different kinds of duck that
live in every kind of watery place, from
river rapids to marshy ponds, and from lakes to
the open ocean. Although these many kinds of
duck have different colours and live in different
ways, they share a similar shape of body
and beak that we all know as –
just duck!